TWENTY-FOUR-

CABINET BOOKS, NEW YORK

Inspired by literary precedents such as automatic writing, by the resourcefulness of the *bricoleur* making do with what is at hand, and by the openness toward chance that all artistic production under severe constraint must necessarily incorporate, Cabinet's "24-Hour Book" series invites a number of distinguished authors and artists to be incarcerated in its gallery space to complete a project from start to finish within twenty-four hours.

Written between 10:00 am, 10 December 2011
and 10:00 am, 11 December 2011

I Am Sitting in a Room
Brian Dillon

No. 1 in Cabinet's "24-Hour Book" series

For Felicity. Infinite riches in a little room.

Brian Dillon is UK editor of *Cabinet* and tutor in the Critical Writing in Art & Design program at the Royal College of Art. He is editor of *Ruins* (MIT Press/Whitechapel Gallery, 2011) and author of *Sanctuary* (Sternberg Press, 2011). His book *Tormented Hope: Nine Hypochondriac Lives* (Penguin, 2009), published in the US as *The Hypochondriacs* (Faber and Faber, 2010), was shortlisted for the Wellcome Trust Book Prize. His first book, *In the Dark Room* (Penguin, 2005), won the Irish Book Award for non-fiction. A collection of his essays, *Culture and Curiosity*, will be published by Sternberg Press in 2012. Dillon writes regularly for *Artforum*, *Frieze*, *Art Review*, the *Guardian*, the *London Review of Books*, and the *Wire*, and is currently at work on *Blown All to Nothing*, the story of an explosion at a gunpowder works in Kent in 1916.

Brian Dillon was born in Dublin in 1969 and lives in Canterbury, England.

Brian Dillon at his temporary desk at Cabinet writing *I Am Sitting in a Room*. Photo taken at 6:19 PM on Saturday, 10 December 2011.

Consider no work perfect over which you have not once sat from evening to broad daylight.
— Walter Benjamin, "One-Way Street"

Chapter 1

IDEALLY, OF COURSE, one would write in bed. The author awakes refreshed and early—among the few infuriating individuals I know who claim to write this way, five o'clock seems the optimum time—and turns his thoughts straight away to the work at hand. There follows a blissful fugue during which words arrive without urging or unease; perhaps they spill out like a natural overflow of the dreams—torrid but ordered, just disturbing enough to be useful and not enough to distract the writerly mind—that he or she has lately left behind. One lies there, or sits propped and pillowed, in a paradoxical state of half-awake alertness. The softness of the notebook pages, the whispery smoothness of the pencil's advance, the laptop's halo dimmed halfway: such things effect just the right sensory introduction to the day, and the writing body feels dry but fluid, acute and suave, perfectly attuned to the task of the next few brightening hours.

And it is—let us be clear (especially today) about what is being envied here—a matter of no more than three or four hours of comfortable productivity. For sure, nature will call: picture the writer pushing aside papers and power cables, padding to the bathroom unimpeded by partner or children (for these few hours, whatever the reality, one lives alone), still with the current sentence held costively in mind as the body relaxes. There might even be coffee or tea, assuming the kitchen is not too far away and the paraphernalia not overly complex. But the job—maybe the writer sighs a little happy sigh, en route back to bed, at the thought that this is a *job*—is to stay suspended in this warm and delicate bubble of real work until, without guilt or regret, one simply stops. After that, any manner of madness or mundanity. The writer acknowledges the presence of spouse or offspring. The writer leaves the house and commutes to a day job. The writer starts drinking. The writer cycles a mile or two to the seashore and swims vigorously for half an hour, thinks about what to do with the day.

———

This is not, assuredly not, my own writing routine. (Though I have written in or on a number of beds, and we will have to return to the scene of the bed-loving and even bed-bound, bed-ridden, author.) A friend tells me that he does indeed cycle to the seaside every morning after typing the day's allotted pages, but I am unsure whether to believe him: there must be days, and I console myself with the thought, when he rolls late from the bed without a word in his head or left behind on the screen, and fetches up at the beach in a state of high anxiety, a tide of unwritten pages rising to drown the despairing authorial ego.

No, what we have here in this *au lit* interlude is one especially fond and idealized version of the writer's spatiotemporal imaginary: a fantasy according to which writing could be allotted its discrete place in the diurnal round and its properly cosseted and open relationship with the material world. Decor, furniture, technology, agenda or calendar, authorial circadian rhythms and the bodies and minds of loved ones nearby: all of it contracts and conspires to produce a delicious ease whose excuse is that it is really a form of rigor, of labor no less. And literary history (which today includes pop-cultural vignettes and questionnaires on the writing life, as well as more or less kitschy author photos of the scribe *in situ*) tells us that such visions, and indeed architectural, DIY-ish, athletic, sybaritic and neurotic efforts at putting them into practice, have not ceased to shadow the production of actual books, poems, essays, and ephemera. Writing, when it happens—it's not always clear that it will happen—happens in a space, among objects and arrangements of things and time that are at once absolutely necessary and dangerously distracting, perhaps ruinous to the whole writing enterprise.

I am sitting in a room, and I am trying to recall and to explore these spaces, these structures, these artifacts. There are the beds, of course, and the bedside consoles of which more below. And the studies, the offices, the huts and sheds, the basement retreats. The tables, desks, antique bureaus, and plain boards placed upon the lap, the portable escritoires and stand-up lecterns for those with the stamina. The café tables, the floors of packed commuter trains, the domestic staircases and jealously guarded portions of kitchens and parlors, these last

Agatha Christie, photographed on 1 March 1946.

either permanently set up for writing or understood to be so set aside for a portion of the day. (Here, in the first of a varied and always slightly precious frieze of author-at-work images that I shall either describe or reproduce, is Agatha Christie in tweed suit and brogues, typing at a drop-leaved oval table. Yes, there are bookshelves in the background, but her writing materials might easily be cleared away in readiness for tea, or the arrival of an inquisitive police sergeant from the local village.) Writing happens in space—it happens to a body, which is in touch with time and things, and which tries to enclose itself and connect itself to real and fantastical outsides, to make itself at home and fling itself abroad in a mobile analogue of home. The question, I suppose, *is what is going on in there?*

———————

Here are some of the places I wrote, or attempted to write, not including (for reasons of present and threatening anxiety, plus the more fretful memories thus awakened) classrooms and exam halls, ca. 1975–1987. A mustard-colored sofa in the house in Dublin in which I grew up—here the trick was to balance on the fat rounded arm of the sofa the small red notebook in which I composed an excessively long book report on a novel by the sentimental Irish children's writer Eilís Dillon, to whom I am not related. A very low desk, intended for a smaller child, at a public library a couple of miles from home. The dining-room table (we only ate at it at Christmas and Easter, or when relatives arrived from abroad) adjacent to bookshelves full of my father's fading orange Penguin paperbacks. Sitting on the end of my bed. I never wrote in that bed, except for one appalling effort at poetry when I was seventeen.

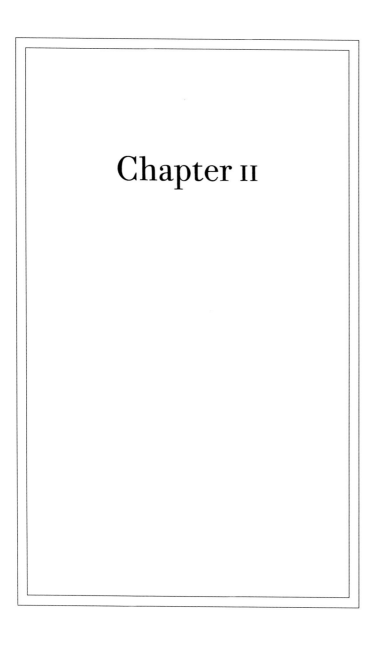

Chapter II

THE WRITER'S STUDY or office is a machine for enclosing the self and at the same time letting the mind wander, and the architectural volume with its props and accoutrements has to do the complex job of actually achieving both while allegorizing or exaggerating those processes so as to convince the writer that they are truly afoot. (Always, while writing, these little tricks to tell myself that I am capable of a task before which I have no choice, but which I could very well walk away from— could walk away from right now, in fact.) The office, in other words, is an apparatus geared towards reassurance. It makes me feel comfortable and adventurous, safe and at the same time the sort of person who might think or feel or write anything at all, such are my portals onto the world and reminders at hand of distant places, histories and people. (Books, of course, but images too and mementos, familiars, charms, amulets).

Here, for example, is St. Jerome in his study: a subject for numerous artists, most famously Antonello da Messina and Albrecht Dürer. (Jerome is typically depicted either sojourning in the Syrian desert or immured in his Latin translation of the Bible.) In the painting by the former, completed around 1475, the saint is ensconced at the center of a ravishing contraption of symbolism and architecture. A stone arch protects and invites us into the scene: the tiled floor of a cathedral, darkened in its upper reaches and giving out onto countryside, houses and open sky where a few glyphic birds are swooping. Perspective leads the eye in several directions—to the left, an open expanse of floor and a cruciform window frame; to the right, a lion stepping delicately beneath a vaulted ceiling.

But it's the object at the center that truly intrigues with its variety of lines and angles and shadowed spaces. Jerome has ascended three steps to a dais or platform at the rear of which are four large shelves sparsely strewn with open books, pottery, and other more obscure objects. (I cannot help thinking they look like the bookshelves of an academic who has just moved into a new office and is awaiting the arrival of his or her library, in the meantime unnecessarily staking a claim.) Two more big shelves at the left are spilling books onto the desk—if that is what it is: maybe the whole thing, the whole building, is a desk?—before which the saintly figure sits, lavishly robed, on a chair that resembles a squat tower.

As Georges Perec notes in a peerless analysis of the painting in his *Species of Spaces*, Jerome is here several times enclosed; the "study" of the title is in fact a nested puzzle, a kind of origami office made of involuting folds of architectural space, at the center of which the scholar thinks and reads and writes. But that is not all. Or rather, the whole edifice has been confected so as to arrive at, to spiral inwards towards, the actual surface

Antonello da Messina, *Saint Jerome in his Study*,
ca. 1475.

on which Jerome's book rests: a shallow slope, some way past the ideal angle for a laptop, built above a curtailed arch. (He could if he wanted to tuck his knees into this arch, in a moment of effort or concentration.) And it is this that seems most telling, or most moving, in this elaborately erudite and spatially complex scene: the writing surface itself looks provisional, half-thought, perilous. All of this careful activity of enclosure and protection has been in the service of something frail and unfinished.

––––––––––

My study (of which, I hope, more later) resembles Jerome's only in this sense: that it is so disposed—that is the wrong word; that it is so strewn—as to leave only a square foot or two in which to work: enough real estate among books and papers and letters and outdated invitations to exhibition openings for an open book and a notebook, or a laptop, or the somewhat awkward conjunction of iPad and wireless keyboard on which I am trying to elaborate these thoughts and at the same time (it was inevitable) remaking this relatively public space in the image of the chaos at home. If I were to go looking for literary analogues for this shameful disorder, of which of course I am secretly proud, it might be in the opening pages of W. G. Sebald's The Rings of Saturn, where the author's semi-fictional stand-in describes the university office of his late colleague

Janine Dakyns: "Years ago, Janine had been obliged by the ever-increasing masses of paper on her desk to bring further tables into use, and these tables, where similar processes of accretion had subsequently taken place, represented later epochs, so to speak, in the evolution of Janine's paper universe. The carpet, too, had long since vanished beneath several inches of paper; indeed, the paper had begun climbing from the floor, on which, year after year, it had settled, was now up the walls as high as the top of the door frame, page upon page of memoranda and notes pinned up in multiple layers, all of them by just one corner. . . . It occurred to me that at dusk, when all of this paper seemed to gather into itself the pallor of the fading light, it was like the snow in the fields, long ago, beneath the ink-black sky. In the end Janine was reduced to working from an easychair drawn more or less into the middle of her room where, if one passed her door, which was always ajar, she could be seen bent almost double scribbling on a pad on her knees or sometimes just lost in thought." Though I have to admit that even this picture of academic squalor, with its invocation of melancholy and Romantic land-scapes of the distant European past, is far, far too lugu-briously attractive as an image of the frank hell in which I have frequently, in the face of ill-managed deadlines, reduced myself to working.

Chapter III

A FEW OF THE PLACES in which I tried to write, and at times if not frequently succeeded, roughly from 1987 to 1995. The kitchen table of the house where I grew up, in latter years used for little except breakfast, writing, and the provisional storage of Eng. Lit. and Philosophy texts. The dark Victorian reading room of another local library (a Carnegie library, as I didn't know at the time), with its precipitously slanting desks and tattered upholstery. The much brighter and noisier library of University College Dublin. (Late on a winter morning in 1988 I leaned too far back in my chair while clutching a desk and toppled the whole arrangement, books and half-written essay and myself, onto the floor.) Two libraries at Trinity College Dublin, and a computer room—it shook regularly as trains passed overhead— where I first tried to write straight to the computer, with typo-ridden and near-disastrous, in terms of academic progress, results. Various cafés. The ground-floor bed-room of a shared house on Cork Street, Dublin: filled during the day with traffic fumes and curses. A similar but smaller room in a house not far away; I wrote next to nothing there.

———

For years, and especially in light of the immediately *supra*, the fantasy of the writerly retreat or cubby hole or (better) hut. This is a populous space: best to admit that the desire is not original, though I was hardly envious of the most celebrated shed-writers. Consider George Bernard Shaw, whose crankish ways—the wearing of wool next to the skin, the somewhat strident vegetarianism, and the labored witticisms, not to mention my long-standing allergy to the writing—seem to lead seamlessly to the specifics of his writing shed in the Hertfordshire village of Ayot St Lawrence. Shaw, it seems, loved nothing better than being photographed, so that we have ample evidence not just of the shed itself, which is anyway still standing, but of his preening Jaeger-clad pride in it. Here he is with the door flung open, squatting on the threshold with a finger raised mock-profoundly to wild eyebrow, deep (apparently deep) in conversation with Vivien Leigh. Or again, possibly from the same session, sitting on a floral-cushioned wicker chair, bent in a Jerome-ish attitude of concentration, fingers on the keys of his typewriter, which conspicuously contains no paper. And most alarmingly, in an issue of *Modern Mechanics* magazine from 1929, photographed at the doorway, aged 72—and heavily retouched: he's outlined like a cartoon GBS—athletically turning the whole building round with one hand. Because this is the most famous fact about Shaw's hut: it was capable of revolving so that the sun-loving writer could keep warm and enthused to the task at hand. The accompanying article assures us that "Mr. Shaw's plan to keep the sun shining on him is a simple health measure, and not a wanton eccentricity."

George Bernard Shaw as Superman, *Modern Mechanics*, August 1929.

Bernard Shaw's Rotating House Is an Aid to Health

George Bernard Shaw revolving his workshop.

A REVOLVING turntable is one of the factors in the splendid health of George Bernard Shaw, famous English author. At the age of 72, he is in the prime of physical condition and attributes it partially to his appreciation of sunlight. Mr. Shaw has a plan to keep the sun shining on him constantly while he works. He has constructed a small hut on his grounds that is built on a turntable. When the morning sun shifts, he merely places his shoulder against the side of the hut and gives it a push so that the warming beams fall through his window at the correct angle.

Mr. Shaw's plan to keep the sun shining on him is a simple health measure, and not a wanton eccentricity.

The house is not a new idea. Several years ago such a building was constructed in France. It was built with glass walls and was equipped with a motor that moved it at the touch of an electric button. The original model cost $50,000. Mr. Shaw's cost much less than $1,000.

The author has spent most of his life out of doors, but when he moved to London he didn't get as much sun as he thought he needed. Hence the hut.

In the canon of writerly retreats, the revolving shed is of course madly if admirably eccentric—I imagine it picking up speed as it spins, finally attaining escape velocity and hurtling away above the Hertfordshire countryside, its owner become a pompous and bearded Dorothy. In fact, we may as well admit this too: there is something insufferable and absurd about the writer in his shed—it is usually *his*; Virginia Woolf's is the exception among great writers of the last century. There is more than a hint of asocialized male retreat and obsessive regard for the mechanics of making oneself comfortable enough to do something as apparently untaxing and even effete as mere writing. What is it about authors in England, especially, that makes them want to take to their sheds? At the time of writing, British newspapers have lately been exercised by the fate of Roald Dahl's equally celebrated shed, where he would slip his lower half into a sleeping bag, recline in an armchair, and place upon his knees a board cushioned beneath (here is the touch of comfort too far) by wads of corrugated cardboard. The shed is at present the subject of some mild controversy: the author's family wishes it not only to be preserved but relocated intact—they are trying to attract public funding—to the Dahl museum in Buckinghamshire, somewhat in the style of Francis Bacon's London studio which was painstakingly gathered up, dust and all, and reconstructed in the Hugh Lane Gallery in Dublin in 1998. This strikes some

Virginia Woolf photographed by Duncan Grant in 1932. Michael H. Whitworth writes: "When she had formally settled down to work, she rarely worked at a table, but sat in a low armchair with a plywood board across her knees. In the late morning or afternoon she would type up what she had thus written by hand."

literary journalists as evincing excessive regard for the ephemera of such a "light" author as Dahl.

———————

So much for whimsical Anglo retreats. The Americans and the Germans do the hut-bound thing with more earnestness, not to say metaphysical import. There is Thoreau, of course, though actually I have never read Thoreau and there is no time now. Instead, let Martin Heidegger stand for the *echt* rural hut-dweller, with his visions of authentic subsidence into the land, into dreams at once of ancient continents and freshly discovered bucolic havens. Here is the philosopher in his hut at Todtnauberg, in the Black Forest: a building of which the scholar Adam Sharr has written: "Heidegger is found to have sustained simultaneously quite different relationships with his hut and house. The former appears closely aligned with his writings' emphasis on the philosophical and experiential potential of human situation. The latter was organized around domestic life, broadly 'aesthetic' in sensibility. There are many ways to interpret Heidegger's hut—as the site of heroic confrontation between philosopher and existence; as the petit bourgeois escape of a misguided romantic; as a place overshadowed by fascism; or as an entirely unremarkable little building." Like Shaw, Heidegger gives in easily to the photographer's instructions, poses meaningfully at his desk and seems entirely of a piece

Roald Dahl in his writing hut, ca. 1990.
Photograph by Jan Baldwin. Courtesy of the Roald
Dahl Museum and Story Centre.

Photograph of Heidegger in his hut taken in 1966 as part of a series of images that were to accompany an interview he had granted to *Der Spiegel*. Photograph by Digne Meller-Marcoviz.

The ruins of Ludwig Wittgenstein's hut
overlooking Lake Eidsvatnet in Skjolden, Norway.
Photograph by Guy Moreton. Courtesy the artist.

Wittgenstein's desk in his residence at
Trinity College, Cambridge. Photograph by Patrick
Lakey. Courtesy the artist and Nye+Brown.

with the grain of the wooden wall behind him.

I prefer, though, to think of Wittgenstein in Norway, holed up in his hut overlooking Lake Eidsvatnet in Skjolden: "In Norway . . . it seems to me that I had given birth to new trains of thought within me." Or in the west of Ireland, sequestered in a cottage at Rosro in Connemara, of which he wrote that he had found "the last pool of darkness in Europe." The melodrama of that last phrase aside, I think I prefer Wittgenstein the homemaker because he seemed capable of inhabiting any interior at all, replicating the space of thought in his rooms at Trinity College, Cambridge, in a glum hotel room on the north bank of the river Liffey in Dublin, or in the midst of a desolation that seems only modestly, rigorously desolate, not so conducive to floridly Romantic seclusion or weighty pronouncements on building, dwelling, and thinking.

———————

From the catalogue of Henley Offices ("garden offices for work and play"), from which I joyfully and more than a little self-consciously took delivery of a Compact Standard garden office in the summer of 2006:

> *The Compact Office Standard at 2m × 3.2m internally, is the optimum size for a one-person workspace. It has plenty of room for regular meetings with up to 3 people and ample storage space.*

... The Compact has a footprint of just over 10 sq metres (including roof overhang) so it will fit into even the smallest of gardens.

Full specified Henley Compact Office Standard
2 m × 3.2 m interior floor space
84 mm insulated walls
84 mm insulated floor
84 mm insulated ceiling
Plastic coated steel roof
3 × double glazed PVCU windows
Key operated window locks
Household quality, PVCU, reinforced door with laminated glass panel
Brass door handle
5 lever door lock conforming to BS3621
3 × double electric sockets
2 × double spot lamps
Fuse Box
All internal cabling
Attractive & hardwearing interior
Marineply cladding treated with premium "Flood"
*   - 5 year no maintenance coating with a choice*
*   of colours*
All exterior items sprayed and pressure treated for long life to BS EN 927-1 1997
Tanalised timber base
5 year structural guarantee

Henley Compact Standard "garden office" installed at Brian Dillon's home in Canterbury, England.

Delivery & installation by our own experienced fitters.

Why wait? Order now and pay nothing for 12 months or £29 a week on a fixed monthly payment plan.

Chapter IV

"I NEED AN HOUR ALONE before dinner, with a drink, to go over what I've done that day. I can't do it late in the afternoon because I'm too close to it. Also the drink helps. It removes me from the pages. . . . Another thing I need to do, when I'm nearing the end of the book, is sleep in the same room with it. . . . Somehow the book doesn't leave you when you're asleep right next to it." Thus Joan Didion, in Jill Krementz's lovely and sometimes funny book of photographs of authors and their workspaces, *The Writer's Desk*. And here is Didion, photographed by Krementz in California in 1972. The bed is just visible in another room behind her, and it's either bare or very neatly made up. Didion sits barefoot in a long dress, looks openly at the camera. A thin trail of smoke, ending in a little spiral flurry, comes from the window-lit desk beside her, but the cigarette is obscured by a truly vast typewriter: a thing of amazing curvy heft and presence, more military in its bearing (shades of Nazi code machines) than the kind of writing tool you might expect to be used by the slight, neurasthenic author of *The White Album*. It is decidedly not the typewriter that Didion describes in the title essay of that book, when she lists the things she takes with her on assignment and invites us to picture her setting up her mobile office: "Note the typewriter for the airport, coming home: the idea was to turn in the Hertz car, check in, find an empty bench, and start typing the day's notes."

I AM SITTING IN A ROOM

Joan Didion, Trancas, California, 1972.
Photograph by Jill Krementz.

I like the idea of Didion at the airport, watchful no doubt, with notes to hand and typewriter on her knees, almost as much as I like the notion that Wittgenstein could be Wittgenstein in any remote destination. (This is different, I think, from the image of the writer merely abroad or traveling: all that silly romance of the likes of Bruce Chatwin with his moleskine, before they were Moleskine, notebooks—I mean, I like the notebooks but not the romance.)

I admire, that is to say, the idea of the mobile, or maybe better the *translatable*, office. The difference seems to matter, now that we carry our working lives around in our bags or pockets: I am trying, I think, to sketch a set of bodily attitudes rather than a collection of miniature technologies, a deliberate and theatrical structure rather than mere convenience or utility. The best description I know comes from Roland Barthes, who in his beautiful autobiography of sorts—a book we all insist on calling *Roland Barthes by Roland Barthes*, though really it is just called *Roland Barthes*—reproduces photographs of himself in three discrete but similar workspaces: in the first he is painting, probably at home in Paris in the apartment on the rue Servandoni that he shared with his mother; in the second he is at his office desk writing by hand, his typewriter (as always) on another desk to his right; in the third, on holiday, in shorts and sandals that sink into a plush white carpet, he is sorting papers on a coffee table. In truth, the "offices" are not that similar, but they must have felt similar, for here is Barthes in 1973, interviewed by *Le Monde*: "To be able to function, I need to be able structurally to reproduce my usual work space. In Paris, the place where I work (every day from 9:30 AM to 1 PM; this regular workaday schedule for writing suits me better than an aleatory schedule, which supposes a state of continual excitement) is in my bedroom. This space is completed by a music area (I play the piano every day, at about the same time: 2:30 in the afternoon) and by a 'painting' area—I say 'painting' with lots of quotation marks (about once a week I perform as a Sunday painter, so I need a place to splatter paint around.) In my country house, I have faithfully reproduced those three areas. It's not important that they're not in the same room. It isn't the walls but the structures that count."

———————

Much as I admire and aspire to the Barthesian structural and mobile office, I have to admit that this semi-fantastical version of the writer's study too can turn precious, even tawdry. Vladimir Nabokov is hard at work on his index cards, or so we're meant to think. In 1959, *Life* magazine dispatched photographer Carl Mydans to Ithaca, NY, to capture the author of *Lolita* in a variety of now familiar Nabokovian poses. Here is the novelist hamming it up in dappled cavort with his butterfly net, strolling in tweeds with his wife Vera,

Roland Barthes in his office in Paris, 1963.
Photograph by Henri Cartier-Bresson.

Vladimir Nabokov writing on index cards in
his car, Ithaca, New York, September 1958.
Photograph by Carl Mydans for *LIFE* magazine.

poised to respond to her latest chess move, lounging alone in bed with a manuscript. Here are the famous index cards themselves, snug and well-thumbed in a cardboard box, paper-clipped into little bundles. And here is Nabokov again, slouched in the passenger seat of a large and palely upholstered car, tortoiseshells on the end of his nose, pretending to write. The caption tells us: "He likes to work in the car, writing on index cards." Which he is patently not doing in the photograph where he stares mock-sternly from the car window, holding a couple of cards in his left hand and a pencil in his right.

(Nowadays, when I think about index cards I am most likely thinking too about Nabokov. Not that I consider index cards very often, still less handle any, let alone write on one. I have a feeling I bought some in the mid-1990s, in a fit of grad-student guilt about the state of my notes (handwritten, my dad's 1940s Schaeffer fountain pen, lined A4 pad), and never used them. It would not seriously occur to me to try and organize on index cards my present, no less haphazard and illegible notes (handwritten, cheap mechanical pencil, unlined A5-ish notebook), though something of the sort would have the advantage of keeping notes and drafts together for discrete projects, thus avoiding that annoying interregnum when you have to carry two notebooks around because you haven't yet finished all the work planned or sort of even half written in the first, now full. Which irritation hasn't stopped me, once or twice in the last decade, buying several small notebooks with the intention of dividing my various responsibilities and writing-related fantasies among them: a short-lived compromise between one big "waste book" (such as employed by the great German scientist and aphorist Georg Christoph Lichtenberg) and the dispersible archive of index cards. Short-lived because pretty soon you catch yourself thinking far too much about this stuff, and resolve to revert to the simplest set-up. As if that is somehow less pernickety, less precious.)

The foregoing parenthesis was maybe written in an effort to stave off thinking about William F. Buckley, Jr., who in 1974 was photographed by Jill Krementz supposedly at work, like Nabokov, in his car. I hesitate, in fact I refuse, to reproduce the image, which you will have to take my word is astounding in its smugness. Buckley lounges, damp-forelocked, on the absurdly plush back seat (there is, believe it or not, some scroll-like stitching) with pen and reading glasses in hand and papers on his knee, cradling a telephone and sidling up to a huge briefcase. A happy dog, spaniel-ish, lolls on the seat's headrest. Here is the caption quote from Buckley, which I will reproduce without comment: "It is a large car. I remember having no exact figure in mind when the manager of the garage in Texarkana asked me how long I wanted it, so I simply extended my legs from the desk chair I was sitting in and suggested it be two feet longer than the current standard model. . . . I use the car constantly. . . . I turn on my Dictaphone, and check to see that the battery is alive. It is. it always is. Dictaphone has managed to construct a portable recording machine which is about the only thing around to remind us that we actually won the war against Japan."

Chapter v

BUCKLEY IS BY NO MEANS ALONE in allow-
ing (maybe encouraging) the genre of the author photograph to go badly awry. Consider the case of Philip
Roth, photographed by Krementz in New York in 1971.
Unlike most of her literary subjects, the novelist dis-
tances himself in the accompanying quotation from
the whole undertaking, practically scorns the photographer's, and the reader's, interest in the quotidian
practices of writers as a breed. "I don't ask writers about
their work habits. I really don't care. Joyce Carol Oates
says somewhere that when writers ask each other what
time they start working and when they finish and how
much time they take for lunch, they're actually trying
to find out, 'Is he as crazy as I am?' I don't need that
question answered." All well and good—at some level I
share Roth's suspicion of the obsessive interest in such
minutiae. But what are we to make of the accompanying image? Here is the author sporting open-necked
shirt and alarming moustache, grinning away as he
leans against his large antique desk in front of his bookshelves and, of all things, his *library ladder*. I don't
believe Philip Roth. I think he's *obsessed* by writerly
impedimenta, and I bet he eyed the other photographs
in Krementz's book with alternate fury and satisfaction.

By contrast, here is Susan Sontag in an author photo
that really ought to irritate. The room is high-ceil-
inged, the desk is hefty, the cigarette fat and short and
therefore probably French, the copy of the *New York*

I AM SITTING IN A ROOM

Philip Roth, New York City, 1971. Photograph
by Jill Krementz.

Susan Sontag, New York City, 1974. Photograph
by Jill Krementz.

Review of Books is angled a little too artfully toward the camera. Are those Gallimard paperbacks stacked four or five deep in front of her? Is Sontag really, I mean *really*, sitting sunlit and assured beneath a lovely vintage advertisement for Olivetti typewriters? It is all too much, and yet: I forgive her. She probably needed this level of awkwardly erudite self-invention, and she does nothing to deny the necessary ruse.

Possibly my favorite author photo of all time: Ernest Hemingway faces away from the camera and writes at his lectern. I don't much care for Hemingway's prose. But look at his legs. One has to conclude that he acquired those calves simply by writing. Writing *very hard*.

The question of the bed: I promised to return to it, to go back to that warm paradise of productivity. The objectively greatest author photograph? It is Man Ray's image of Proust dead in the bed where he had worked, surrounded by the paraphernalia of his childhood and gilded youth and heroic middle age: the books, the photographs, the medicinal powders, the notebooks and loose papers on which, in the full knowledge that he was dying, he had labored on, the MS of his novel held aloft over his prone and laboring body, like (in Walter Benjamin's beautiful image) Michelangelo at work on

Ernest Hemingway flexing his literary muscles.

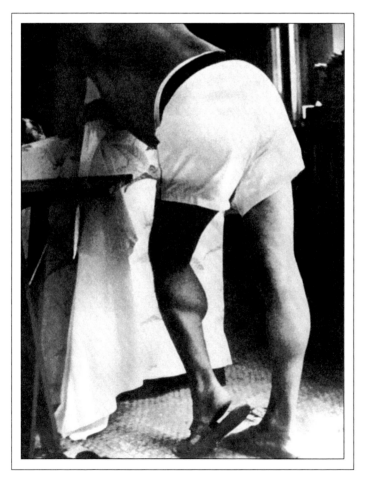

Mark Twain at work in his bed, ca. 1900.
Courtesy Barrett Collection, Special Collections,
University of Virginia Library.

Marcel Proust no longer at work in his bed, 20
November 1922. Photograph by Man Ray.

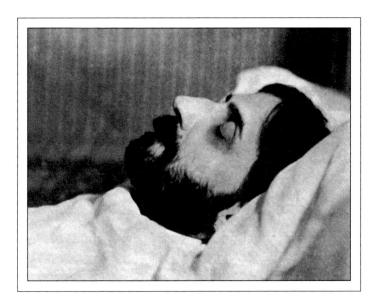

the ceiling of the Sistine Chapel. I can do no better, in sketching the end of his struggle, than to quote his servant, Céleste Albaret: "As I came up to the bed he turned his head slightly toward me, opened his lips, and spoke. It was the first time he'd ever spoken to me immediately on waking up and before having had his first cup of coffee. And it never happened again. I couldn't help looking surprised. 'Good morning, Céleste,' he said. For a moment his smile seemed to savor my surprise. Then: 'A great thing happened during the night.' 'What, monsieur?' 'Guess.' He was enjoying himself. . . . So I said: 'I don't see what it can be, monsieur, I can't guess. It must be a miracle. You'll have to tell me.' He laughed like a boy who has played a trick on someone. 'Well, my dear Céleste, I shall tell you. It is great news. Last night I wrote "The End."' And then he added smiling, and with that light in his eyes: 'Now I can die.'"

Chapter VI

HERE IS A PARTIAL LIST of the places I have written since 1995. A cramped room in a university hall of residence in Canterbury, England. The bedrooms of various shared houses to which I escaped after the hall of residence. The front bedroom of a tiny cottage in the village of Herne, Kent. A larger bedroom of my present house in Canterbury. A dilapidated summer house at the end of the garden of the same house: I wrote my first book there and only abandoned it when late on a December evening in 2004 I glanced up from my desk and saw a field mouse shivering as it clung to the curtain. The shed, of course, which replaced the summer house. In bed in a borrowed sixteenth-century cottage in Sussex. The Gulbenkian Library at the University of Kent, Canterbury: the worst library I have ever used and by far the worst to write in. I have the feeling this place ruined me for writing in libraries forever; hitherto pretty much the only places I had ever managed to finish substantial projects, they now became overheated dens of distraction and anxiety. But I carried on dreaming of the perfect library, and so: the British Library, the London Library, the archive at Tate Britain, the National Archive—I've succeeded in writing the odd paragraph in these places, but nothing impressive. Various cafés, with mixed results. I've tried writing in hotel rooms in London, Dublin, New York, Berlin, Seoul, Basel, Los Angeles, and Paris—doubtless elsewhere too—and succeeded once, maybe twice. I think I may give up trying to write in hotel rooms.

———————

On the wall just above and to the right of my desk in the beloved shed—the shed which I have been treating badly and now resolve to tidy when I get home—I have in recent years stuck a number of pink and orange Post-It notes on which are penciled quotations I like to believe (and it's true) will get me through the writing day, get me over those frequent moments of modest, never truly tragic or crippling, writer's block. Let me be clear: I never use Post-Its for anything else. Like index cards, they seem a relic of the early 1990s: a pre-laptop, pre-iPad, also pre-Moleskine era. I must have bought the pack of notes alongside the index cards on moving from Dublin to Canterbury in the autumn of 1995. Their continued adhesive power is remarkable—maybe their sticking to things for years is a point of pride among Post-It execs and the gum-fingered adhesion engineers who do their bidding—and only weakened once they are on the wall, when the heater below dries them out and they need periodic pressing and smoothing back in place.

The quotations are not exactly talismanic or aphoristic or even the most essential I would think of if asked to cobble together a small canon of writerly advice. But they have served their modest purpose, and seen me through four books and several hundred essays and articles. They seem, and are, very far away right now, and I reproduce here just the few whose more or less accurate wording I can recall:

To substitute metaphor for the concept: to write.
    — Roland Barthes

There is no order outside the order of the material.
    — Robert Smithson

There is a delicate empiricism which so intimately involves itself with the object that it becomes true theory.
    — Goethe, via Walter Benjamin

I am at war with the obvious.
    — William Eggleston

Most of them sit at home at their PC *and in a bone-headed way fiddle around with their things, and most of the time the result is something very anaemic.*
    — W. G. Sebald

Sometimes it's better not to have the whole story.
    — Nina Katchadourian

Theodor Adorno, *Minima Moralia*, trans. Edmund Jephcott (London: Verso, 1985).

Roland Barthes, *The Grain of the Voice: Interviews 1962–1980*, trans. Linda Coverdale (New York: Hill & Wang, 1986).

Roland Barthes, *Roland Barthes*, trans. Richard Howard (New York: Hill & Wang, 2010).

Walter Benjamin, *One-Way Street and Other Writings*, trans. Edmund Jephcott and Kingsley Shorter (London: Verso, 1979).

Bill Berkson and Joe LeSueue, eds., *Homages to Frank O'Hara* (Bolinas, CA: Big Sky, 1988).

Mary Ann Caws, *Virginia Woolf* (New York: Overlook Press, 2004).

Joan Didion, *The White Album* (New York: Simon & Schuster, 1979).

Diana Fuss, *The Sense of an Interior* (New York & London: Routledge, 2004).

A. M. Gibbs, *Bernard Shaw: A Life* (Gainesville, FL: The University Press of Florida, 2005).

Irvin Haas, *Historic Homes of American Authors* (Washington, DC: The Preservation Press, 1991).

Stephanie Kraft, *No Castles on Main Street: American Authors and Their Homes* (Chicago, New York, and San Francisco: Rand McNally & Company, 1979).

Markus Krajewski, *Paper Machines: About Cards & Catalogs, 1548–1929*, trans. Peter Krapp (Cambridge, MA: The MIT Press, 2011).

Jill Krementz, *The Writer's Desk* (New York: Random House, 1996).

Vladimir Nabokov, *Speak Memory: An Autobiography Revisited* (London: Penguin Classics, 2000).

George Perec, *Thoughts of Sorts*, trans. David Bellos (Boston: Verba Mundi, 2009).

Sally Peters, *Bernard Shaw: The Ascent of the Superman* (New Haven: Yale University Press, 1996).

W. G. Sebald, *The Rings of Saturn* (London: The Harvill Press, 1998).

Adam Sharr, *Heidegger's Hut* (Cambridge, MA: The MIT Press, 2006).

David G. Spielman, William W. Starr, and Fred Hobson, *Southern Writers* (Columbia, sc: University of South Carolina Press, 1997).

Michael H. Whitworth, *Virginia Woolf* (Oxford: Oxford University Press, 2005).

Saturday, 10 December 2011

10:32 AM Earl Grey tea with milk
10:51 AM cigarette
12:01 AM cigarette
12:03 PM water
1:47 PM cigarette
*2:20 PM BLT sandwich, duck rillettes on bread,
    coffee with milk, one chocolate biscuit*
3:18 PM cigarette
5:10 PM coffee with milk
5:29 PM two chocolate biscuits
5:33 PM cigarette
*8:38 PM pork dumplings, sesame chicken with
    white rice, seltzer*
10:54 PM cigarette
11:11 PM coffee with milk

Sunday, 11 December 2011

1:05 AM cigarette
*6:23 AM Two eggs, roll, one banana, one apple,
    plain yogurt, vanilla yogurt, coffee with milk*
8:19 AM cigarette
9:14 AM cigarette

I Am Sitting in a Room
Brian Dillon

Design: Everything Studio
Research and assistance: Madeline Hollander,
Claire Lehmann, Samuel Shuman.
Editors: Jeffrey Kastner & Sina Najafi

Cabinet wishes to thank the Interdisciplinary Doctoral
Program in the Humanities at Princeton University
(IHUM) for its collaboration on this project. Additional
thanks to Ben Kafka, Patrick Lakey, and Guy Moreton,
and Felicity Dunworth for texts, phone calls, everything.

ISBN: 978-1-932698-54-1

Printed by BookMobile, Minneapolis, USA.

Published by Cabinet Books
Immaterial Incorporated
181 Wyckoff Street
Brooklyn, NY 11217 USA
<www.cabinetmagazine.org>

Cabinet Books is the book imprint of Immaterial
Incorporated, a non-profit 501(c)3 organization whose
core activity is the publication of Cabinet magazine.